For Royston William Smith (1928–2000),
his family, and for all families touched by Alzheimer's
R. W.

In memory of Margaret Anelli
L. A.

First U.S. edition 2018
First published by Penguin Random House Australia Pty. Ltd. 2016

Library of Congress Catalog Card Number pending
ISBN 978-1-5362-0138-3

18 19 20 21 22 23 LEO 10 9 8 7 6 5 4 3 2 1

Printed in Heshan, Guangdong, China

This book was typeset in Utopia.
The illustrations were done in collage, mono print,
watercolor, and acrylic and colored digitally.

Candlewick Press
99 Dover Street
Somerville, Massachusetts 02144

visit us at www.candlewick.com

ROSS WATKINS

ILLUSTRATED BY LIZ ANELLI

DAD'S CAMERA

CANDLEWICK PRESS

Dad came home one day with one of those old cameras, the kind that uses film.

He said nothing about it, though. He just
took the camera from its box, put it to his eye,
and walked into his study.

My study is my brain, he always said.

Dad had his ways.

Dad started doing more funny things, like putting
things that belonged in the fridge in the cupboard
and things that belonged in the cupboard in the fridge.

The doctor told Mom this was part of the process
and said to expect more of the same.

He's simply becoming forgetful, Mom explained to me.

But Dad didn't take photos of the regular things
people photograph. . . .

Mom asked him why he didn't want to take
a photo of us, but he wouldn't say.

He just put the camera to his eye, pointed it at his cereal bowl, his coffee cup, and clicked.

Dad took photos of the things he didn't want to forget.

When Dad finished his first roll of film, he took it to an old store in the city to be developed. He came home with a thick envelope under his arm, went straight into his study, and stuck the photos across the window.

Dad finished another roll.

Then another.

And another.

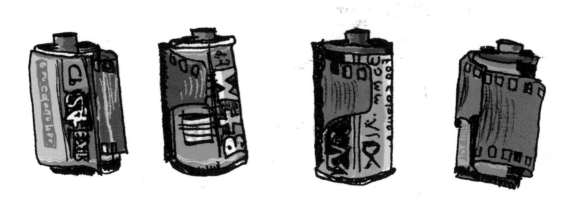

When Mom saw the window almost full
with the photographs, she yelled at him.
Aren't we worth remembering? she said.

Dad just looked confused, and I reminded
her about him forgetting things.

Which included us.

Which made us cry.

But Dad came home one day without
the camera. We assumed that he'd simply
put it down somewhere and forgotten it.

Then we lost Dad.

Not long after, we received a box in the mail.
The handwriting on the label was Dad's,
and inside the box was Dad's camera.

We took out the camera, walked into
his study, and placed it on his desk.

He should be here, Mom said.

But then, by the afternoon light of the window,
in the space he left behind,
we noticed that there was still film inside the camera.

We took the film to the old store
in the city and had it developed.

I don't see the point, the man said.

We didn't understand.

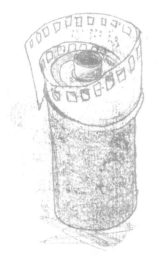

There's only one photo, he said.

Then he opened the envelope and he
showed us the photo and we smiled.

Sometimes, one is enough.

And now we see. And now we know.
Dad took photos of the things he
wanted *us* to remember . . .

about him.